I Want a Hat Like That

Illustrated by Tom Cooke

Featuring Jim Henson's
Sesame Street Muppets

A Random House
PICTUREBACK® Shape Book

CTW Books

 Published in the United States by Random House, Inc., New York, and simultaneously in Canada by Random House of Canada Limited, Toronto, in conjunction with Children's Television Workshop. Originally published by Golden Books Publishing Company, Inc., in 1987.
First Random House edition, 2000.
Library of Congress Catalog Card Number: 99-61343 ISBN: 0-375-80438-2
www.randomhouse.com/kids www.sesamestreet.com
Printed in the United States of America January 2000 10 9 8 7 6 5 4 3 2 1

I want a hat like that.

I, Grover the trick rider, will perform on my trusty tricycle.

I want a daredevil helmet.

I, Grover the sailor, will sail the ocean blue.

I want a sea captain's hat.

I, Grover the detective, will follow the clues just like Sherlock Hemlock. I want a detective's hat.

I, Grover the football player, will run with the ball on the Sesame Street Cyclone team. Go, team, go!

I want a football helmet.

I, Grover the construction worker,
will build tall towers.
I want a hard hat.

I, Grover the astronaut, will blast off into space.

I want a space helmet.

10, 9, 8, 7, 6, 5, 4, 3, 2, 1—MOMMIEEEE!

I, Grover the cowboy, will ride in rodeos. Whoa, boy!

I want a cowboy hat.

I, Grover the artist, will paint a portrait of my friend.

I want an artist's beret.

I, Grover the baseball player, will throw a super-fast ball.

I want a baseball cap.

I, Grover the fire fighter, will fight forest fires.

I want a fire hat.

I, Grover the actor, will star in a play.
I want a costume hat.

I want a hat like that!